For Mum, with thanks for all her efforts to turn us into real girls …

BLOOMSBURY
CHILDREN'S
BOOKS

First published in Great Britain in 2000 by Bloomsbury Publishing Plc
38 Soho Square, London W1V 5DF
This paperback edition first published in 2001

Text copyright © Vanessa Gill-Brown 2000
Illustrations copyright © Mandy Stanley 2000
The moral right of the author and illustrator has been asserted.

A CIP catalogue record for this book is available from the British Library.
ISBN 0 7475 5038 7 (paperback)
ISBN 0 7475 4469 7 (hardback)

Designed by Dawn Apperley

Printed and bound by South China Printing Co.

5 7 9 10 8 6

Rufferella

Vanessa Gill-Brown and Mandy Stanley

BLOOMSBURY
CHILDREN'S
BOOKS

Diamante loved stories and her most favourite was Cinderella. She liked to imagine that she was the fairy godmother – the one who made things happen. She desperately wanted to turn something into something – but what?

One day, her eyes rested on Ruff, her dog – aha! She would turn her dog into … into … a human, into a Ruff-erella!

'How about it Ruff?' she exclaimed. 'Want to be a girl?'

Ruff didn't fancy being a human much. But Diamante could be very convincing, and soon, Ruff was sure it was all trifle and television in the human world. But how would it happen?

They didn't even have a magic wand.
  'I don't need one,' said Diamante confidently. 'I will teach you how to be human. It isn't difficult. I do it all the time without even thinking.'

So the lessons began.
First Diamante dressed
Ruff in human clothes,

did her hair in a human
style and applied some
human make-up.

'There!' she squealed. 'At least you look like a real girl now! And you shall be called Rufferella.'

Next Rufferella learned how to eat with a knife and fork, drink from a cup and how to cough and sneeze politely.

Diamante also tried to explain about not taking all the chocolate biscuits for yourself, but Rufferella found this aspect of being human very difficult to swallow (unlike the chocolate biscuits).

Look at it her way – finally allowed to eat human treats and she was supposed to let others choose first? Sausages in particular would have posed a problem – Ruff loved those more than anything.

Diamante decided to show her off at a friend's birthday party.
  'You shall go to the ball, Rufferella! Well, Penny's party,
anyway. But you mustn't let anyone know you're really a
dog.'

Rufferella was nervous,
but she had no need to be.
She danced, played
games, drank pop, ate
cake and all without
spilling a drop or a crumb.
She even sang happy
birthday to Penny.

To everyone's delight she had the most beautiful, deep voice anyone at the party had ever heard.

'What a wonderful voice this girl has – she should be on the telly!'

After that, she was invited to sing at
other people's parties, then in theatres,
where crowds came to hear the
amazingly sweet, low voice of little
Rufferella. And eventually she did
sing on the TV.

The ball was wonderful. Everything was bright and
sparkling and beautiful. Everyone wanted to dance with
Rufferella and compliment her on her charming – and
unusual – singing voice.

So Diamante replied to the Queen, accepting her kind invitation and they both set about getting new dresses and hair-do's.

One day, among the usual heap of post for Rufferella, a very special invitation came. Diamante opened it.

'It's from the Queen! She saw you on telly and wants you – and a guest – to attend a ball at the palace! You really are Rufferella!'

'Splendid,' said Rufferella.

Diamante always went with her, but she couldn't help feeling a bit left out. There was no time for playing football or rolling around on the carpet, like they used to. Still, it was fun being Rufferella's assistant.

After that, she was invited to sing at other people's parties, then in theatres, where crowds came to hear the amazingly sweet, low voice of little Rufferella. And eventually she did sing on the TV.

To everyone's delight she had the most beautiful, deep voice anyone at the party had ever heard.

'What a wonderful voice this girl has – she should be on the telly!'

Rufferella was nervous,
but she had no need to be.
She danced, played
games, drank pop, ate
cake and all without
spilling a drop or a crumb.
She even sang happy
birthday to Penny.

Diamante decided to show her off at a friend's birthday party.
  'You shall go to the ball, Rufferella! Well, Penny's party,
anyway. But you mustn't let anyone know you're really a
dog.'

Next Rufferella learned how to eat with a knife and fork, drink from a cup and how to cough and sneeze politely.

Diamante also tried to explain about not taking all the chocolate biscuits for yourself, but Rufferella found this aspect of being human very difficult to swallow (unlike the chocolate biscuits).

Look at it her way – finally allowed to eat human treats and she was supposed to let others choose first? Sausages in particular would have posed a problem – Ruff loved those more than anything.

Ahem.
Atishoo!

'There!' she squealed. 'At least you look like a real girl now! And you shall be called Rufferella.'

So the lessons began.
First Diamante dressed
Ruff in human clothes,

did her hair in a human
style and applied some
human make-up.

They didn't even have a magic wand.

'I don't need one,' said Diamante confidently. 'I will teach you how to be human. It isn't difficult. I do it all the time without even thinking.'

Ruff didn't fancy being a human much. But Diamante could be very convincing, and soon, Ruff was sure it was all trifle and television in the human world. But how would it happen?

One day, her eyes rested on Ruff, her dog – aha! She
would turn her dog into … into … a human, into a
Ruff-erella!

'How about it Ruff?' she exclaimed. 'Want to be a girl?'

Then they were escorted to the dining room.

Rufferella was worried – Diamante's place was miles away.
She'd never been totally on her own before and she was
hungry. And the prince next to her was just a tiny bit
stupid and boring and the dress was just a little bit tight …
    She wondered what was for dinner. She watched as the
Queen was served. It was sausages. SAUSAGES!!
Rufferella took one look and leapt on to the table,
bounding towards the Queen.

Rufferella landed in the Queen's plate and began wolfing the delicious, juicy sausages.

'Good heavens, she's a DOG! Rufferella is a dog! No wonder she had such an unusual singing voice. Catch her!' exclaimed the people. Then Rufferella took another flying leap, this time landing in Diamante's arms. Together, they ran out of the palace and all the way home.

Next morning, there was less post than usual, but there was a parcel for Rufferella. She was feeling miserable and didn't want to look at it. So Diamante opened it and took out something hard, wrapped in tissue. There was a note with it which read:

Dear 'Rufferella'

Please do not worry about the unfortunate events at the ball, (sausages are hard to resist after all). A little piece of royal advice: one is often best off if one allows one to be oneself. By this I mean that while I make a reasonable job of being Queen, I should make a pig's ear of being a popstar.

Take care dear
Queen

Diamante unwrapped the item.

   'It's a dog's bowl!' she cried. Rufferella was so pleased that a tear came to her eye.

   'Can I use it?' she asked. 'If it's all the same to you, I think I'll give up being a human, and my singing career. It's just not me.'

'Oh, good,' replied Diamante, 'I've really missed having you as my pet.'

Ruff smiled and said, 'No more Rufferella?'

'No more Rufferella,' agreed Diamante.

'Fancy a trip to the park to play with the old ball?' asked Diamante. Ruff yelped in agreement and off they went.
Everything was back to normal.

Acclaim for this book

'A piece of bright, girly fun, in eye-grabbing pinks and oranges' *The Scotsman*